Mishi's Magic World

By Carla Martilotti

Mishi's Magic World
All Rights Reserved.
Copyright 2012 by Carla Martilotti.

ISBN-13: 9781686986925

Mishi's Magic World

by

Carla Martilotti

Mishi is a beautiful, many-colored cat who lives in a magical world. She loves to enjoy different, wonderful journeys of magic.

Today, she got up and went to have her delicious breakfast, very important to start the day so she can have all the energy that she will need to play and enjoy what was awaiting her.

After she finished her breakfast, she sat for a while and thought, "What do I want to do today? It looks very beautiful outside." So, she started walking towards the garden door.

"Oh, what a wonderful day!" she said. "The garden looks so nice with all these flowers and trees and caves made of stone. I'm going to have a marvelous day!"

She decided to walk towards the nearest cave, which the gardener built especially for her. They were made from stones and dirt that connects one part of the garden with another.

She entered the cave, walking very slowly and carefully (as cats do when they are curious about something).

She walked for a while when all of a sudden she saw a very sparkly light at her right side.

She stopped, looked and could not believe what she saw! It was a beautiful group of small creatures, dancing around!

"Meow! What is this?" Mishi said aloud.

One of the creatures responded to her:

"We are the fairies of the imagination. And we heard that you want to have a special adventure today. So we are here to help you and have fun with you!"

"YES!" Mishi said. "What can I do?"

"Well," the fairy responded, "let's start with what you want to do."

"Since you are fairies," Mishi said, "I want to enter into a magical world."

"Okay!" the fairies said. "Let's go!"

Mishi kept walking with the fairies through the garden when she suddenly saw a lake and mountains and beautiful trees to climb.

She was so full of excitement that she decided to jump into a big tree and climb to the top.

So, she did! And all of a sudden, she realized that the tree was soooooooooo tall that when she looked down from it, she was too scared to climb back down!

So, she meowed very loudly once, twice, three times, and then something happened… the tree *spoke to her!*

"Don't be afraid," he said, raising his branches (which are the arms of a tree), grabbing Mishi and placing her into another set of branches, and so on and so forth until she was on a branch right near the ground.

Mishi was fascinated! "I did not know that trees could talk and move their arms like that!" she said excitedly.

She looked at the tree and became more amazed when she saw the tree looking back at her with his two big eyes and a big smile upon his face.

She stopped. "I didn't know that you have a face!" she exclaimed.

The tree looked back at her and said, "Well, you didn't, Mishi, because you never took the time to look at me and find my face."

"Hmmm…" Mishi said. "That is true, I did not, but from now on, I promise you, I will!"

So, she gave the tree a big hug and kept walking.

She was so happy, and then she suddenly stopped.

"What is this?" she said. "It looks like a stone, but why is it moving? And what are those things on the top of it? It looks like a drawing or something."

She decided to touch the stone, and when she did, it moved up towards her. She jumped with surprise! Then the stone suddenly grew a neck and a head, and the head of that stone suddenly said, "I am a turtle."

"A turtle?!" Mishi said.

"Yes, that is my name!" the turtle replied.

And then Mishi sat to talk with the turtle, which walked a bit towards her and said, "You never saw a turtle before?"

"No," Mishi replied. "And what is that you have upon your back? It looks like someone drew something on you!"

"Oh, no," the turtle said. "This is very important. Would you like to know all about it?"

"Yes! Yes!" Mishi said, so the turtle sat and told her his story.

"This is my house," he said. "This is where I live. And these things on my back, well, these drawings are part of a legend.

"There was an emperor who was sitting one day by a river, when he suddenly saw a big turtle that had very beautiful designs on its shell. To the emperor, the designs looked like the sky and the stars, like a magical thing upon her back.

"So we loved the emperor's thoughts so much that the story became very important to us."

"Oh, meow," she said. "I will come back to visit you every day so that I can learn more about you. Goodbye!"

Mishi was very happy with all of these new things that she was learning, so she started walking once again, when she realized that a little pond lay right before her.

You know that cats do not like water very much, so she began to avoid the pond by walking around it. It was then that she saw her reflection in the water, so she stopped and looked at it.

All of a sudden, the water began speaking to her and said, "Do not be afraid. My name is Diamond, and I am very important for you."

"You are?" Mishi asked.

"Yes," the water said. "I am the major source of life for every living thing."

"Yes?" Mishi replied.

"Oh, yes," the water said. "You have so much of me within your body, even if you cannot see it."

"Oh, meow!" Mishi said, and she touched the water with her paw, and this time she liked it! So, she spent some time grooming herself with the water from that beautiful pond.

Now she was clean and happy... time to keep walking! So she did.

As she was walking and smelling the flowers, she saw a beautiful yellow flower turning her head towards the sun.

Mishi stopped and walked towards the flower and asked her, "How is it that you move like that? I have never seen a flower looking at the sun before!"

"Oh, yes," the flower replied. "My name is Sunflower, and that is how I got my name."

"Wow," Mishi said. "Sunflower is a beautiful name. But why do you want to look at the sun like that?"

The sunflower looked at Mishi with a big smile and said, "We, the flowers, need the sun to grow big and beautiful. That's why we love the sun so much.

"The plants need the light of the sun because the sun lights up our days, and when we turn our heads towards the light of the sun, we can see the air dancing. We see little sparkles of light dancing in the air, little shiny things. They are the rays of the sun, you know?"

"The air dancing? Wow! You flowers are very special."

"So are you, Mishi," the sunflower replied. "You are such a good and sweet cat."

"Meow, thank you!" Mishi said, happy to have talked with the flower and knowing her story. And with that, she left.

Mishi was tired, so she decided to relax for a while and went to a very mushy and wonderful pile of grass to do so.

And with her beautiful white belly facing the sun, she fell asleep.

She dreamt of all the beautiful, mysterious things that she had seen that day.

When she awoke, she asked herself what other happy, fun adventures were awaiting her! It was dark, so she decided to walk back home for a nice dinner, and on the way back, she passed by the pond once again.

And to her surprise, it was not her reflection that she saw this time, but the moon and a few stars were instead within the water!

"Oh, meow, what is this?" she said.

The pond recognized her voice and said, "Mishi, I am glad you are still here! These are my night friends, the moon and the stars."

"Oh, but I always see them in the sky. How come they are here with you?" Mishi asked.

"Well," Diamond answered, "they come every night to play with me. They are my friends, and I'm sure that they are yours, too."

"Yes, I think so," Mishi replied.

"Yes," Diamond responded. "Talk to them."

"Okay," Mishi said, and introduced herself to the moon and said, "You look very beautiful tonight."

"Thank you," the moon replied. "I like to brighten with my light my best friend, our planet Earth."

"Our planet?" Mishi said.

"Yes, the planet on which you and all your friends live," said the moon.

"You don't live here, right?" Mishi asked.

"No," the moon replied. "I am close to you. I am your moon, and even though I do not live here, I do visit you with my light each night."

"Oh, that I know," Mishi replied. "I see you every night in the sky. It's wonderful." She then turned her head a little said 'hello' to the stars.

They responded back: "Hi, Mishi!" And Mishi asked them, "You don't live here either, right?"

"No," they said, "but together with the moon, we visit you every night and brighten your sky."

"Oooooohhhh," Mishi said. "And you are close to our land, the Earth?"

"No, but we can still brighten the sky for you to see it every night."

"Oh, this is wonderful," Mishi said. She was so happy with all of the new things that she saw that she could not wait to tell the fairies all of the news.

When she arrived to the back door of her house, she looked around.

"Where are you?" she called aloud to get the attention of the fairies.

"We are here," they replied.

"Oh," Mishi said. "You should know all of the things that I saw today!"

"Yes, we know," the fairies said.

"You know?" Mishi asked.

"Yes, we were with you," replied the fairies.

"You were with me all the time?" Mishi asked.

"Yes," the fairies said. "We are always with you. We always take care of you and watch out for you. That's why you should always tell us what you really want, and if it is good for you, we will make it happen."

"Oh, meow, MEOW!" Mishi said. "This is certainly the best day that I've ever had! Thank you all!"

"Yes," the fairies responded, "it was a very magical day, and so it will be tomorrow. Good night."

So, the next day arrived, and it was a beautiful morning. Mishi looked out the window to begin her usual walk in the garden. While she was doing that, she saw the reflection of herself in the sliding glass door that connected the house to the garden.

"Ooooh... what do I see?" she said to herself. "I have a crown! I had never seen that before on my head! What a beautiful crown... it's very brilliant! I love it!"

She was very happy, thinking of her crown, when she rcalized that she was already by the pond with which she was so familiar.

She looked at herself one more time, and there it was, reflected in Diamond, a beautiful, brilliant crown!

"Meooooww!" she exclaimed. "Diamond, do you see what I see? Do you see my crown?" she said, jumping up and down excitedly.

"Yes!" Diamond responded. "I always see it on you. It's bcautiful!"

"You have always seen it?" she asked.

"Yes," the water responded. "You didn't know?"

"Nooooo! How come I never saw it?"

"I don't know, but you always have had it," Diamond said.

"Oh, meow!" she said all happy, saying goodbye to Diamond and then kept walking towards the big tree. She was so happy with her beautiful crown!

"Mr. Tree," she said. "Do you see something different on me today?"

"No, Mishi, you are so beautiful as always," Mr. Tree said.

"No, no, NO! Don't you see something on my head? Don't you see my crown?"

"Your crown?!" Mr. Tree replied. "What I see is what I always see: it's your beautiful halo, or rainbow."

"A halo? A rainbow?" Mishi said, confused. "Those are the names of my crown?"

"Yes, but you can call it a 'crown' if you want to," Mr. Tree said.

"But what is a halo, or a rainbow?" she asked.

"Oh, you don't know?" answered the tree. "Well, many of us have one."

"Really?" Mishi exclaimed.

"Oh, yes," said Mr. Tree. "You never saw it before?"

"No," Mishi said.

"Don't worry," said the tree. "Remember how the sunflower taught you about how the rays of the sun make the things bright and even the air dance?"

"Oh, okay," Mishi said. "I love it! This is beautiful! Now I understand!"

"Yes, it is," said the tree. "Because you became such a wonderful little cat, you can keep your beautiful crown."

"Oh, thanks!" Mishi replied.

So Mishi kept walking to see if her friend the turtle was nearby. She needed to know if he knew about the crown… well, the halo…

And there he was, the turtle with the sunflower. Both were talking about something.

"Hello, both of you," Mishi said. "Do you see something different on me today?"

"Well, let's see," the turtle said. "You have the same beautiful, shiny hair as always. Hmmm…"

The flower interrupted. "Do you have a new collar?" it asked.

"A new collar?! No!" Mishi said. "I don't have a new collar, but look at my head!" she said, jumping around. "Do you see something on my head?"

"Do you mean a hat?" the turtle asked.

"No, not a hat!" Mishi responded. "A halo, or a crown!"

"Oh, do you mean that?" said the turtle. "I'm happy that you already learned about that, Mishi."

"Ah," the sunflower replied, all happy. "I was telling her the other day about the sun and the sparkles and how wonderful the sun is for all of us, and how the energy from the sun's rays makes the air dance around with beautiful, different colors. So that's why she can see her crown."

"I'm happy that you taught me all of this," Mishi said, smiling.

"And that explains why you have a halo, or a rainbow, atop your head," the sunflower said.

"Yes," Mishi said.

"What were you doing lately?" asked the turtle.

"Well," Mishi replied, "I was walking a lot in the gardens. At the night, I saw the reflections of the moons and the stars, and I also was walking under the rays of the sun. And, as you already know, I was talking to all of you and learning a lot of new things about life and nature."

"See?" the sunflower said. "Because you spent so much time with us and nature, you became wiser!"

"That's more or less what Mr. Tree said," Mishi thought to herself.

"Can you see the colors of the halo?" the turtle asked.

"Yes, they are blue and pink," Mishi said happily.

"You got it!" the turtle said. "There are also some greens and violets and gold… it's really beautiful! Your crown is like when you see a rainbow in the sky, and a rainbow is the crown of the planet."

Mishi was so happy. "Thanks!" she said, waving her tail. "I'm going to keep walking. It's a beautiful day, and I feel verrrrrrry lucky."

"Bye-bye," the turtle and sunflower said together. "We'll see you soon!"

Mishi spent the rest of the day playing and having fun, and when the day started getting darker, she decided to walk towards the house, knowing that she was being accompanied by the fairies all the way.

And therefore, they knew all about the discovery of her crown. She was happy; the fairies had kept their promise of giving her what was good for her and the gift of enjoying a magical world.

"Ooohhh… there is my house!" Mishi thought to herself happily. "I can't wait to have a good night's sleep so that I can start another day of adventure tomorrow, and to give a big hug of thanks to the fairies for all that they did for me!"

And with those thoughts, she went into her house and went to her cozy and beautiful bed, where she fell asleep with a big smile of happiness upon her face.

THE END…???

Other books by author Carla Martilotti

Mishi's Vacation

Pinky Pig: Lost in the City!

Pinky's Birthday

Pinky Pig Meets Farmer Bob's Niece

Pinky's Race

Alice's New Doll

Herbie the Bee

The Little Lizard

Mitten the Kitten

Mitten the Kitten in Shadowland

Made in the USA
Las Vegas, NV
28 January 2021